Tempted at Midnight

The Midlife Crisis Series
By
Rose Bak

Table of Contents

Copyright

TEMPTED AT MIDNIGHT

© 2024 by Rose Bak

ALL RIGHTS RESERVED. No portion of this book may be reproduced, transmitted, downloaded, decompiled, reverse engineered, or stored in or introduced into any information storage retrieval system in any form by any means without express permission from the publisher, except as permitted by U.S. copyright law. For permissions contact the publisher at rosebakenterprises@msn.com.

Warning: the unauthorized reproduction or distribution of this copyrighted work is illegal. Criminal copyright infringement, including infringement without monetary gain, is investigated by the FBI and is punishable by up to 5 years in prison and a fine of $250,000.

This is a work of fiction. Names, characters, places, and incidents are either the product of the author's imagination or are used fictitiously. Any resemblance to actual persons, living or dead, events, organizations, or locals is entirely coincidental. Trademark names are used editorially with no infringement of the respective owner's trademark. All activities depicted occur between consenting characters 18 years or older who are not blood related.

Cover by Aila Glass Designs

About This Book

She's a single mom on the wrong side of forty. He's a single dad with a mission: convince the love of his life that they won't turn into pumpkins when the ball drops at midnight!

Lillian

My kids are away for the weekend, so my best friend convinces me to come to Houston for a New Year's Eve party. I'm a blue-collar worker busy raising three boys not some cartoon princess, but with a makeover and a new dress, I sure feel like one! There's even a handsome prince, but when the sun rises on New Year's Day, I realize he isn't who he said he was.

Martin

When I wake up alone after the best holiday of my life, I can't figure out what went wrong. Fortunately, fate brings me back into Lillian's path, and after I convince her that I wasn't lying to her, we begin to navigate the complexities of dating as single parents. But we live in different towns and have very busy lives, making it almost impossible for us to have couple time.

For this to work, we're going to need a lot of patience, a little creativity, and some intervention from our kids.

"Tempted at Midnight" is an opposites attract midlife romance with a strong and independent woman, a man who believes in love at first sight, six rowdy but sweet kids, and a factory full of nosy matchmakers who are determined to help their friend find love.

Join My Mailing List

Join Rose Bak's mailing list at bit.ly/RoseBakNewsletter[1]. You'll get a free book and be the first to hear about all the latest releases and special sales.

---

1. https://d.docs.live.net/ae511949052ccd53/Documents/bit.ly/RoseBakNewsletter

Dedication

For all the single moms who long to find a clean bathroom, some time for themselves, and someone who loves them just the way they are.

Lillian

I breathed through my mouth as I dumped a load of Logan's dirty clothes into the washing machine. Was there anything stinkier than teenage boys? If so, I wasn't sure what it was. I couldn't figure out how a kid who spent twenty minutes a day in the shower – sometimes longer – still had this much body odor.

He had a gift, my kid did.

I guess I couldn't complain too much. As a single mom to three teenaged boys, things could be much worse. I'd raised all my boys to stay out of trouble, to be respectful, to help around the house, and most importantly, to work hard in school so they could go to college. I didn't want them to spend their entire life working in a factory like me. I wanted those boys to get the hell out of the small town of Kenilworth, Texas and make something of themselves. I was determined to give them the opportunities that I'd never had.

"Mama! We're headin' out."

Luke, my oldest at eighteen, thundered down the basement stairs, closely followed by sixteen year old Lincoln and the baby of the family, fourteen year old Logan. They were all tall and lanky with the sandy blonde hair and blue eyes they'd gotten from their father.

It was pretty much the only thing they'd gotten from him. Brad was twelve years older than me and had swept me off my feet when I was twenty-three years old. A year later I was married and pregnant, with three boys coming in six years. Unfortunately, Brad was a shit husband who spent most of his time drinking beer and watching television when he wasn't at work.

Logan had just turned two when I learned about his daddy's other hobby – sticking his dick in every willing woman he could find. I divorced his ass and when he tried to leave me penniless, I sued him for child support and ownership of the house that I'd paid for almost entirely with my own salary.

I might have worked at a factory, but it was a union job, and I made more than my husband did. That was just another thing that irritated him about me.

During the divorce, Brad petitioned for weekly visitation rights with the boys, and twelve years later we were still waiting for that to start. We hadn't seen hide nor hair of him since the ink dried on the divorce papers. The only reason I knew he was still alive was because the state kept sending me the child support money that they garnished from his paycheck every month.

It made me smile every time I saw the deposit in my bank account, mostly because I knew that it would make him furious every time he looked at his paystubs.

"You've got the directions?" I confirmed.

"Yep," Luke said. "I programmed the address into the GPS on my phone."

"Y'all have your phones and chargers, clean socks and underwear?" They all nodded. "Logan, you got your inhaler?"

My youngest rolled his eyes. "Mama, you don't have to worry about us. You know Aunt Sue and Uncle Lewis are gonna take good care of us."

My brother and his wife lived in Houston, and they'd invited the boys to go with them on a New Year's trip down to Padre Island. My brother won the use of a giant beach house in some contest at his job, and they figured they'd turn it into a family vacation. Lewis and Sue had two boys, one right between Luke and Lincoln, the other between Lincoln and Logan, and all five had grown up thick as thieves.

I'd been invited to go to Padre with them, but I have to admit that I'd been eager to have some time to myself for the first time in I couldn't remember how long. Plus I could pick up a lot of overtime at the factory this week with so many people taking vacation between Christmas and New Year's.

As much as I was looking forward to some 'me time', I was still going to miss my guys. I rushed forward and pulled them into a group hug until they all drew back with a groan.

"We're gonna be okay, Mama," Luke told me in his deep voice. "But will you?"

It was cute how protective he was of me. I was really going to miss him when he went away to college in the fall.

"I'll be fine, sweetie. Y'all have a good time and stay out of trouble. Don't speed. Don't talk back. Don't fight. And remember to put the toilet seat down."

"Yes, Mama," they all chorused.

Then, with a stampede of footsteps, I was alone. My phone rang not ten minutes later.

"You're still coming, right?"

My friend Becky and I had planned a girls' weekend for New Year's. We'd grown up together, but she'd relocated to Houston a while back. We still talked every day and got together whenever we could.

The factory was closed from the Saturday before New Year's until the Tuesday after, and with my boys out of town, it was a good opportunity to have some girl time. I'd grown up a tomboy with three brothers and then had three boys of my own, but I still liked a little pampering every now and again.

"I wouldn't miss it for the world," I promised Becky. "I'm already packed. I'm on shift until eleven Saturday night, then I'll head out Sunday morning."

"Be here by noon," Becky ordered. "I made us a spa appointment."

"I don't need to go to a spa," I protested.

"Well, you're getting a spa day for your Christmas present," she said. "We're going to get dolled up and hit the town. I was invited to a huge party with some people from work, and I have it on good authority that the place will be crawling with single men."

I groaned. "The last thing I need is a man."

"Lillian, you haven't had sex in so long you've probably got cobwebs up in your coochie. We'll put on some fancy clothes, do some flirting, and if the opportunity presents itself, you're gonna get yourself some action."

"I don't have any fancy clothes," I reminded her. "The last time I wore a dress was for my wedding."

"Don't worry, I'll take care of everything. You just get down here."

Martin

"I'm not really up for a whole New Year's Eve thing."

"I don't care," Maria told me, her tone stubborn. "You haven't gone out to do anything fun in forever, and I need a wingman. You, big brother, are my wingman for this party."

I let out an exaggerated sigh, but the truth was, I couldn't deny my sister anything. She did so much for me, in many ways putting her life on hold to help me with the kids, and it wasn't like asking me to go to a New Year's Eve party was that big of a request.

"Fine, but I'm not wearing a tux." The last time I'd worn a tux was for my wedding, and we all knew how that had turned out.

"You don't need a tux," Maria said. "Just wear a suit and a nice tie. Something bright and festive."

"Fine. I'll wear the tie with the Christmas trees on it."

Three hours later I was pulling into the Houston Ambassador Hotel. The stately old hotel reeked of money and status and was the site of tonight's hot ticket event, an invitation-only New Year's Eve party. It was hosted by a group of friends who owned one of the city's most successful tech companies, and you had to know the right people to get in. My sister knew the right people – she was a contractor for the company, working on their social media accounts.

As I walked around the lavish ballroom at my sister's side, I realized that the wingman argument was just a ploy to keep me from sitting home alone on New Year's Eve. Maria did not need me to accompany her, not when she seemed to know half the people here.

"You tricked me," I whispered as we waited in line for the bar. "You didn't need me to come with you at all, did you?"

Maria sent me a smug smile. She looked adorable in a red party dress with a skirt that flared out around her thighs. I'd seen several men giving her appreciative glances, but I had a feeling that her on-again off-again boyfriend was going to be the lucky one tonight. They'd been eye-fucking each other ever since we got here.

As if I'd manifested him, Scott joined us at the bar.

"These shoes are so uncomfortable," someone whispered behind me. "I don't know why I let you talk me into wearing them."

"Because you can't wear steel-toed boots with such a sexy dress," her companion whispered back. "Quit being such a baby."

Subtly I turned around, as if I was checking out the crowd, then my breath sputtered in my chest as I saw her. She had long brown hair that was pulled into some kind of fancy side swept ponytail. In the light, I could see glints of red in the strands.

Her dress fit her like a glove, silver and sparkling with an asymmetrical design that provided a tempting flash of pale skin courtesy of a mesh cut-out right over her right breast. Her arms and legs were strong and muscular, her stomach flat between her curvy hips. My eyes traveled upward past long sparkly earrings and a mouth that was a little too wide for her face to meet amused brown eyes.

"Like what you see?" she teased. Her voice was smooth like velvet.

"I do," I said honestly. "Very much."

She seemed surprised at my response. I reached out a hand. "Hi, I'm Martin."

She shot a quick look at her friend before taking my hand. "Lillian."

I heard a little gasp as our skin touched. Clearly she'd felt that tingly feeling the same way that I had. We stared at each other like we were in some old-time movie.

"Lillian, I must know you. Can I buy you a drink?" I finally asked.

She held up a half-filled glass of wine. "I'm good. But I'd love a dance if you're up for that."

I grabbed her drink and mine, shoving them both at my sister, then took my new love's hand.

"I think they're playing our song."

The woman I was going to spend the rest of my life with laughed as we made our way towards the crowded dance floor.

"Do those kinds of lines usually work for you?" she teased.

I shrugged. "I don't know. The truth is, I don't get out much."

"Neither do I," she admitted as I pulled her into my arms. "What made you come tonight?"

"Other than fate?"

She rolled her eyes, then pinned me with a look that made me want to spill all my secrets.

"My sister wanted me to be her wingman," I said.

"She seems like she's doing okay without you," she noted, drawing my attention to a table near the dance floor. Maria was sitting on Scott's lap, making out with him like they were teens at prom.

"Why don't you get out much?" I asked.

"It's a long, sad story." Lillian gave me a wry smile.

"Well, we've got all night."

Lillian

I came awake in degrees as awareness penetrated the fog of my exhausted sleep. The sun was shining brightly through the sheer drapes on the window, bathing the room in light. There was a thick arm wrapped around my middle, which was kind of a problem because I really had to pee. The arm was attached to a naked man who was sound asleep and snoring softly.

I allowed myself a minute to take him in. He was tall and lean, with the rounded shoulders of a swimmer. A light layer of hair covered his chest, tapering off near his belly button leaving just a line of hair pointing to a very large and very erect cock. Martin was a good-looking guy, with a square jaw that was now covered in stubble, firm lips, a slightly crooked nose, and when he was awake, soulful brown eyes. His dark blond hair was sticking up in all directions against the pillow, probably as a result of my fingers pulling the strands.

The last twenty-four hours had been some of the strangest of my life. I'd arrived in Houston and gone to the spa with Becky, where I'd allowed her to convince me to get red highlights in my normally mousey brown hair. I had to admit though, it really looked good. I'd been exfoliated and had my eyebrows plucked and even gotten my first mani-pedi.

I hadn't done that much grooming for my wedding.

Then Becky had shown me the dress she wanted me to wear, a short, tight sparkly thing that somehow fit my body like it had been made for me. She claimed that she'd bought the dress for herself, but it didn't fit her and she hadn't gotten around to returning it. I strongly suspected that was just an excuse. My friend and I were nowhere near the same size.

Since I was clueless about most female things, Becky did my make-up for me, giving me a smoky eye and dark red lips, then loaned me a pair of strappy high heeled sandals that pinched my feet but made my legs look fabulous.

I'd never been what anyone would call a 'girlie girl', and normally I didn't give a whit about dresses and make-up, but it was nice to be pampered for once. When I looked in the mirror before we left the house, I didn't even recognize myself.

I'd felt like Cinderella at the ball, especially after I agreed to go home with a handsome prince after only a few dances. I wasn't promiscuous, and the truth was I couldn't even remember the last time I had sex, but something about Martin made me throw all caution to the wind.

It was a good choice. The second we hit the front porch of his place we'd started kissing, hardly coming up for breath the entire way back to his bedroom. He'd tossed me on the bed like a caveman, then ate me out until my eyes rolled back in my head and I begged him to stop. We'd had sex three, no four, times throughout the night. It was like we couldn't get enough of each other.

I'd never once had an experience like this. I mean, I liked sex fine, but I'd never had sex this incredible. It was like the difference between the generic coffee I bought in a can and the special whole bean blend my sister-in-law brought me from a coffee farm in Hawaii one time. There was no comparison.

But, like that delicious Hawaiian coffee, this was a one-time thing. Although maybe I could get a quickie from Martin before I took off. One for the road.

Finding my clothing on the floor, I got dressed and headed across the hall to the bathroom. I'd visited it last night, but I'd been too eager to return to Martin's bed to do more than pee and get out.

I took care of my bladder then opened the medicine cabinet, searching for some toothpaste. I didn't have a toothbrush on me – I certainly never expected to have a one-night stand – but maybe I could at least do a finger brush so I didn't knock poor Martin over with my morning breath.

The Mickey Mouse toothbrush in the cabinet caught my attention first. What the hell? I turned and pulled back the shower curtain, finding several kids' toys set up along the ledge, and some fancy shampoo and conditioner that I somehow doubted belonged to a man. At least not a straight man.

My stomach churned as I quietly slid open a drawer in the vanity, finding a curling iron, hair dryer, and several hair ties. The drawer below was filled with face creams and a make-up bag. A large box of tampons was under the sink next to the extra rolls of toilet paper.

Holy. Shit. Had I slept with a married man? Martin never mentioned anything about a wife or kids the entire night. Was he stepping out on them while they were out of town or something? What a jerk.

I tiptoed into the living room, finding a variety of kids' toys in a small box next to the sofa. A half-finished Lego structure sat on the coffee table next to two video game controllers. There was a framed family photo on the mantle. I picked it up, seeing that it was Martin with a woman and three small boys at Disney, the Magic Kingdom castle behind them. They looked happy.

Bile rose up in my throat. I'd just done to another woman what multiple women had done to me all those years ago: slept with someone else's husband. Oh my God.

I debated my options. Should I go wake up that cheating asshole and give him a piece of my mind? Grab a knife from the kitchen and do a home castration?

In the end, I grabbed my purse, rushed out the door, and called for an Uber while waiting around the block. It was just my luck that the first time I did something wild and crazy, it went badly for me.

***

Three weeks later...

"What's this meeting about?" I asked as I dropped into a chair between my coworkers and friends George and Leo.

"I don't know, I never pay attention," George said.

George had a unique ability to tune out everything around him while still looking like he was present. I had no idea how he did that.

"It's something about the new benefits package they're offering," Leo said from my other side.

He was a grizzled older man who'd worked here longer than any of us. He probably should have retired years ago, but no one had the heart to push him out and force him to stare at the walls of his empty house. Leo always told us that he'd probably drop dead right here at Thomas Industries. I had a feeling that he was right. At least he'd go among friends.

"Hey guys, how is everyone today?" David Watson, one of the company vice presidents, strode to the front of the room wearing a nicely pressed suit. He was kind of a tool, the kind of guy who'd never gotten his hands dirty in his life, but we all tolerated him because he was married to George's sister, Josie.

I didn't bat an eye at the 'guys' comment. After growing up with most of these men and being the only woman on shift, everyone considered me one of the guys. Even me. Manufacturing wasn't really a field that attracted a lot of women.

"We brought you here today because we have a presentation on our new benefits package, including some important changes to your retirement plan."

Everyone in the room groaned, and David waved his hands placatingly. "It's all good, I promise. Union leadership supports it as well."

He looked up as one of the secretaries from the main office led in another guy in a suit. Something about him looked familiar. He was tall and lean, with dark blonde hair...oh crap. As he turned, I could see it was Martin, the married guy I'd slept with on New Year's Eve. What were the chances?

I slid down in my chair, and grabbed George's arm, pulling him towards me.

"What's wrong?" he asked.

"Hide me," I whispered.

There were two great things about George. First, he was the kind of friend you could call and tell that you killed someone and he'd come over with a shovel, no questions asked. Second, he was built like a small mountain, so when he leaned in front of me, he blocked me from sight.

I slid to the floor on my knees and kept my head down as Martin talked about our retirement plan, then segwayed into a discussion about changes in our health insurance.

"And for those of you who need birth control...," Martin stopped awkwardly, apparently noticing that everyone in the room was male.

"That would just be Lillian here," Jimmy called out from behind me. "Why you sittin' on the floor, Miss Lillian?"

Everyone turned in our direction and I felt my face flame, which really pissed me off because I wasn't one who was easily embarrassed.

"Lillian?" Martin's voice turned curious. "That's an unusual name."

With a deep sigh I scooted back onto my seat, elbowing George so he'd lean back onto his own side. There were ten rows of chairs between us, but I could see Martin up there, clear as day, staring at me like I was a ghost.

I tipped my chin in acknowledgement, then returned my gaze to the back of Bobby De Lacroix's bald head in the seat in front of me.

"Martin?" David prompted.

After stuttering for a second, he picked right back up on his speech and answered questions from the assembled group, although his eyes kept moving in my direction. Even without looking directly at him, I could feel his gaze on me.

Needless to say, I didn't ask any questions. I just wanted this meeting to end so I could get back on the line and lose myself in the monotony of my work.

When I got out of the room without seeing any more of Martin, I called it a win. Avoiding the curious looks from my friends, I headed to my station to get to work without a word.

Martin

"This shift ends at four?" I asked David with forced casualness.

"Yeah, but you already spoke at second shift yesterday, remember?"

"Oh yeah, of course."

It was better to have David think I was a moron than wonder why I was really asking. I couldn't help myself but to try to pump him for information. I'd damn near fell over when I realized that Lillian was one of the workers here.

She looked so different than she had New Year's Eve, with her hair braided down the back of her head, wearing a faded tee shirt and ratty old jeans. There was no hint of the sophisticated lady I'd danced with and then taken home, but every day Lillian was no less alluring.

When the guy in the audience said her name, I knew immediately it had to be her. There weren't a lot of Lillians out there, and the entire time I'd been speaking at the meeting I'd felt this weird kind of buzzing in my body, like something big was going to happen.

And then it did.

If Lillian sneaking out when I was sleeping without so much as a goodbye or a 'here's my number' wasn't enough of a hint, her hiding to avoid seeing me sure was. Not to mention that when I finished my presentation, she'd run out of the room like she was being chased by hellhounds.

She didn't want to see me, that was clear. Except now that I knew she was here, now that I knew where to find her, I wanted to talk to her. I needed to talk to her.

We'd had what I thought was the perfect night. I'd taken one look at her at the party and fallen half in love with her. By the time I sank into her heat the first time I was fully in love with her. I didn't have a ton of experience with women, other than my ex-wife, but I was absolutely certain she'd felt something that night, same as me.

What had I done wrong?

I borrowed a conference room in the admin suite, telling David I needed to do some work before I made the drive back to Houston, then snuck out of the building a few minutes before four to hang out by the employee entrance. I'd seen it yesterday when I took a wrong turn.

I leaned against the concrete wall facing a sea of concrete parking lot while doing deep breathing exercises and telling myself I was doing the right thing waiting to talk to Lillian. It just didn't make sense, her running away like that.

At precisely five minutes after four o'clock, employees started streaming out of the building. A few minutes later Lillian walked out with the giant man who'd been sitting beside her in the meeting. I hoped he wasn't her boyfriend because there's no way I could take that guy.

"Lillian."

Her back stiffened as she heard my voice. She stood stock still for a long moment before turning slowly to face me. The hulk beside her stopped as well, and so did two other guys, closing ranks around her.

The look she gave me was less than welcoming, but I couldn't look away from her natural beauty.

"Hey Lillian, could I talk to you for a minute? Please?"

Her face flushed with anger. "I have nothing to say to you, Martin."

I was so confused. Why was she mad at me when she was the one who'd disappeared?

The men around her looked between us curiously but didn't interfere. Clearly they thought she could hold her own. Taking my life in my hands, I stepped closer to their little group.

"I just...why did you leave me like that?" I knew I sounded like a pussy, but it had been killing me, not knowing what happened.

"I thought most guys liked it when a woman didn't hang around the morning after a one-night stand?"

Her entourage all looked surprised, like it had never occurred to them that she'd do something so wild. I took another step closer. Her eyes looked troubled and maybe a little hurt.

"I'm not most guys. I, uh, I thought there was a connection there. We had fun."

"Do you have fun with your wife too?" she snapped.

Her voice was cold and hard, nothing like the sweet and fun woman I'd held in my arms. The three guys protecting her snapped to attention at her question, each of them looking like they were fixing to cut me.

"What are you talking about? I don't have a wife," I protested.

"That's funny, because your house was filled with kids' toys, your bathroom had a bunch of girlie shit in it, and there was a picture of you and your family on the fireplace mantle. It looked like y'all were having a grand old time at Disney World."

I was starting to realize what had gone wrong. Damn it, we'd never got around to talking about our personal lives, what with all the fucking we'd been doing. She must have woken up, looked around my house, and jumped to all the wrong conclusions.

"I have three sons," I started.

"Oh my God, just like you," the younger guy who'd outted her in the meeting laughed like it was the funniest thing he'd ever heard.

I waited for Lillian to meet my eye.

"Lillian, I don't have a wife. I mean, I did have a wife, but she ditched us several years ago. My sister Maria, the one you saw at the party, she lives with me to help out with the kids. It was her stuff you saw."

"The woman in the picture was a redhead," she said suspiciously. "Your sister had dark hair."

"Maria changes her hair color every few months," I explained. "Seriously, look."

I pulled out my phone, opening my photo app and shoving it in her direction. "Look through my phone, you'll see the pictures."

She thumbed through the pictures at a quick pace, eyes coasting over pictures of my sister and my kids while the hulk guy stared over her shoulder suspiciously. Finally Lillian handed the phone back to me, her expression less angry and more uncertain.

"How do I know you're not making all this up?" she asked. "I never talked to that woman you said was your sister. You guys could be swingers or something."

"You think I have time to be a swinger with three kids and a full-time job?" I asked incredulously.

"He makes a good point," the older guy noted. "You're always tellin' us that you're too busy to comb your own hair let alone date. I don't see you havin' time to be a swinger either."

She rolled her eyes. "Thanks, Leo."

"No problem. Now are you gonna hear this here fella out, or what?"

Lillian

Ignoring Leo's smart comments, I stared hungrily at Martin. God, he looked good. He was wearing a navy suit with a white shirt that was open at the collar, revealing a triangle of skin just below his neck that I knew tasted delicious.

Could I have misunderstood what I saw at his house? And more importantly, did our time together mean as much to him as it had to me? Because I, for one, could not stop thinking about it. I'd damn near worn out my vibrator the last few weeks replaying it in my mind.

Then I remembered that I was a middle-aged single mom and I didn't have time for romance. My midnight temptation was a one-time thing. Even if I wanted to spend more time with Martin, my life was much too crazy to date.

"Why are you waitin' for me?" I asked gruffly.

"Can we go somewhere and talk?" he asked softly. "I'll buy you a drink."

I was tempted to mention that the last time he got me a drink I'd wound up face down over his bed while he pounded into me from behind, but I wasn't about to bring that particular image up in front of our audience.

"I have to get home for my kids," I lied.

"Your kids aren't home yet, Lillian," Leo said in his disappointed father voice. "And them being home ain't never stopped you from getting' a drink with us."

I turned and gave him a glare that would have hobbled a lesser man before returning my attention to Martin.

"I guess I might could have a quick drink," I said grudgingly.

The wide smile on his face was gratifying.

"There's a bar about a mile up the road called LJ's, I'll meet you there in a few minutes."

"Sounds good. Thanks."

As soon as he walked away, Jimmy and Leo were on me with questions, while George just looked on, as was his way. He was as nosy as the rest of them, but he wasn't one to be obvious about his prying.

I held up my hand to forestall the deluge of questions.

"Y'all remember my friend Becky?"

They all nodded since everyone knew everyone in this town.

"I went to Houston to spend New Year's Eve with her, and she insisted that we get dressed up and go to this fancy party. I met Martin there, we clicked, then I woke up the next morning and started thinkin' he was married with kids. I left while he was asleep, and today's the first time I've seen him since."

I held up my hand again. "I will not be accepting any other questions at this time, and if any of you show up at LJ's to spy on me, I'll knee you in the balls so hard you'll be coughing them up outta your mouth. Got it?"

They all looked a little green, probably because they knew I'd do it.

"See y'all tomorrow."

Martin was waiting for me on the sidewalk when I pulled up at LJ's. It was a great little dive bar where we often stopped by for a drink when we got off shift. Martin held the door for me and I walked in, calling out a greeting to Chrissy, one of the servers here.

She hustled over, her curious eyes taking in Martin's suit and neatly combed hair. This was strictly a blue-collar establishment, and they didn't get a lot of fancy looking guys in here. I'd never seen any of the suits from factory administration in here, other than David every now and again.

"Hi there, I'm Chrissy. What can I getcha?"

Martin nodded for me to go first.

"I'll have a bottle of Lone Star, Chrissy."

"I'll have the same," Martin said.

"You want a basket of fries?" Chrissy asked.

I smiled. My love of fried potatoes was well-known. "Yep, you know I do. Thanks."

We sat quietly until Chrissy brought our beers, then Martin spoke up.

"I was really bummed when I woke up and found you gone, Lil."

I ignored his shortening of my name even though it was kind of sweet.

"It was a one-night stand, we both knew the score going in," I reminded him. "Even if I hadn't discovered what I discovered, it's not like I was gonna move in with you and live happily ever after."

"Why not?"

I looked at him like he was nuts.

"Because that wasn't really me, Martin. The make-up, the fancy hair, the cute little dress. This is the real me."

I waved my hand up and down in front of myself.

"My shoes have steel toes, my hair's a mess, my jeans are older than at least one of my kids, I'm wearing a sports bra because they're more comfortable for work, and I smell vaguely of machine oil. The Lillian you danced with at midnight doesn't exist in real life. She's a fantasy."

"I don't want a fantasy. I want you."

Martin

Lillian was looking at me like I was crazy. I needed to downshift this conversation before she ran away screaming.

"All I'm saying is, we had fun together, and we have a connection that doesn't come around every day. How about we date? We'll go out a few times and get to know each other better. Maybe even have more of that incredibly hot and wild sex we had on New Year's."

An older guy in khakis and a sweater walked by at that exact minute, his head snapping around so fast to look at Lillian. I was surprised he didn't break his neck.

"Hey Mr. Williams."

She rolled her eyes at me as the man ambled away.

"That was my high school algebra teacher. I can guarantee you that I'll be getting a message from my mother asking who you are within the hour."

"Wow, small town life, huh?"

"Yeah."

"So you grew up here, and you work at Thomas Industries, and you're a mom...tell me more."

She hesitated long enough that I thought she wasn't going to answer, but then she took another drink of her beer, gave me a considering look, and gave me the highlights.

"I grew up here, the only girl out of four kids. I always wanted to go to college, but I couldn't afford it, so after I graduated high school I applied for a job at the factory. I think they were trying to prove that women couldn't do the work or some shit, because they hired me and spent a good year hazing me. But I grew up being harassed by dumbass boys, and this wasn't no different. Once I proved myself, things got better. I learned a lot over the years, and most days, I really like my job."

"What do you like about it?"

She smiled her thanks as the waitress set down a basket of fries, chewing one thoughtfully before answering. I studied her lips until I realized I was getting hard and had to look away.

"It's the kind of job I can do and go home and not think about it. That's perfect for me. I want to clock out and be done so I can focus on my boys."

"You have three, I heard?"

"Yeah. Typical story. I married young, got swept off my feet by a handsome charmer. He knocked me up three times in six years, all the while keeping a couple of other girls on the side. When I found out I kicked his ass to the curb. Haven't heard from him since."

I frowned. "He's not involved in your kids' life?"

"Nope, he wanted to punish me for suing him for child support, so he abandoned his boys. Never showed up for one pick-up day ever. Eventually I went to court to rescind his visitation rights, now he can only see them if he gets permission from me. He's never asked, not once in twelve years. I don't know that my boys would even recognize him if they saw him walkin' down the street."

"Jesus."

I stuffed a handful of fries in my mouth to keep from saying what was really on my mind. I had no respect for a man who abandoned his kids. Then again, I'd been married to a woman who'd abandoned hers.

Lillian saw right through me. "It's okay, I came to terms with it a long time ago. Brad is an asshole, but it's his loss really. My boys grew up to be awesome young men."

"How old are they?"

"Luke just turned eighteen, Lincoln is sixteen, and Logan, he's my baby, he's fourteen. Now what about you?" she asked. "What's your story?"

"Well, it's really not all different from yours, I guess. I was born and raised just outside of Houston," I started. "I waited until I turned thirty to find the love of my life, then when she didn't show up, I convinced myself that Amy was that person. She wasn't. The physical side was good, at least at first, but after we had three kids, she was done."

I drained the rest of my beer and gestured for the waitress to bring me another.

"She was...unhappy in our marriage. Unhappy being a mother. She used to always tell me that I'd ruined her life and killed all her dreams by marrying her, and that the kids had ruined her body. One day she announced that she wanted out, she told me that she wanted to live the life she was always meant to have. I suggested that we go to marriage counseling, but instead she left divorce and custody papers on the nightstand and moved out that same day. She's living in Dallas now from what I hear."

My words were neutral, belying all the pain behind them. I still felt guilty about Amy to this day, wondering if I'd pressured her too much, or if I'd been a bad husband. I guess I'd never know. I only knew that once she was gone it was clear to me that I'd never loved her, not the way a husband should love his wife.

"At least I got my boys out of the relationship," I continued. "But they were young when she left, and a handful, so my sister volunteered to move in and help with them. The woman is a saint."

"How old are your boys?" Lillian asked.

"They're twelve, ten, and eight, spaced out at two-year intervals just like yours. They keep me on my toes, for sure."

"Martin, I really like you, but you've got your life in Houston, and I've got my life here. That doesn't give us much opportunity for crossover," Lillian said sadly. "It's probably best we say goodbye, cuz I'm not seein' this going anywhere."

I grabbed her hand, wrapping my fingers around hers. Everywhere our skin touched sizzled. A pulse was hammering frantically in Lillian's throat, and her eyes were wide and confused.

She was right, things between us would be complicated, but it wouldn't be impossible.

"I'm sorry, I don't accept your rejection," I said firmly.

She pulled her hand back. "What? You can't reject a rejection!"

"Sure I can."

Her mouth opened and closed a few times, but nothing came out.

"If I thought you weren't interested Lil, I'd walk out that door and never come back again. But you're looking at me like you're thinking about me naked, and I'd bet my last dollar your panties are damp right now. So no, I'm not going to accept your rejection. Single parents date all the time. We just need to figure out how to make it work."

Lillian

"See? I told you this wasn't going to work."

We were standing in the parking lot at LJ's, skimming through our calendars trying to figure out when we could have a date. With two jobs and six kids between us, it wasn't easy.

"Hush, we'll figure something out. What about next Friday night?"

I shook my head. "Luke and Lincoln have a football game. Saturday?"

"Karl has a taekwondo match. Unless you want to go with us?"

I shook my head. "As romantic as that sounds, I'm gonna have to take a pass."

"Saturday night?"

I stared at our family calendar, coming up blank. "There's nothing on the calendar..."

"Ding ding, we have a winner. Don't move, let me text my sister and make sure she can babysit."

He thumbed out a quick text and the answer came back almost immediately.

"Maria is good. That's it, we are going on a date in..." he looked at his phone again, "ten days."

Martin grabbed my phone out of my hand. "What are you doing?"

"Exchanging phone numbers," he said.

His phone beeped in his other hand, letting me know that he'd texted himself from my phone. I laughed when I looked at the entry.

"Did you seriously put yourself in my phone as 'Handsome Stud'?" I asked.

He nodded. "It seemed fitting."

My phone vibrated with a message from Lincoln asking what we were doing for dinner and complaining that he was starving. I hadn't realized how much time had passed while I'd sat in LJ's talking to Martin.

"I gotta go," I told him regretfully. "My boys are getting hungry, and they get a little crazy when that happens."

"One more thing before you go..."

Before I knew what was happening, Martin backed me up against the driver's side door of my SUV and was kissing me like he was a dying man and I was his last meal.

My toes curled in my steel-toed boots as I slid my arms around his waist and pulled him closer. He tasted like beer and French fries and something that was uniquely Martin. I'd never felt like this before. No man had ever kissed me this intensely, this thoroughly, and no man had been able to get me this close to an orgasm without even moving his hands below my waist.

When he pulled back, his erection was pressing against my belly and my breath was coming in short pants. It took everything in me not to suggest we make use of the back seat of my car.

"Wow," I whispered.

He gave me a smirk. "Yeah. You see why I couldn't accept your rejection?"

"Yeah."

He leaned forward and gave me a closed mouth kiss, leaned back, then did it again. It was sweet. Damn it, I really liked this guy. Sure, I was more attracted to him than I'd been to anyone in my life, but I liked him too.

And that exactly the thing that was going to get me in trouble someday.

The next day the guys were on me the second I got to work. I hadn't even clocked in before they started with the questions.

"Didja get lucky last night, Miss Lillian?" Jimmy smirked as I put on my safety glasses and headed onto the floor.

"Yeah Jimmy, I fucked him right in the middle of the parking lot at LJ's, then I dry humped him in a booth while we were waitin' for our beers."

Even behind his safety glasses I could see his eyes widen comically. "Really?"

I smacked him on the back of the head. "No, you idiot. I swear your mama dropped you on your head too many times."

"What did you two do then, young lady?"

I hadn't even heard Leo come up behind me. I smirked at his calling me 'young lady' given that I was firmly in my forties.

"We had a drink and talked while we shared a basket of fries, then we both went home to our kids."

"You gonna see him again?" This was from George.

"We have a date planned for next Saturday night, are you nosy old ladies happy?" They all nodded. "Great, then let's get to work."

At some point during my time at Thomas Industries I'd become the de facto den mother of this crew, and their sudden interest in my personal life was unsettling. Usually, I was the one asking them questions and giving advice. Then again, I didn't usually have a personal life for them to be interested in.

Like most single mothers that I knew, I spent all of my time working to support my kids, driving them around, and trying hard to raise them to be upstanding citizens instead of sociopaths. I think I was doing a pretty good job, but the more I thought about it, the more I realized my friend Becky was right. Now that my boys were getting a little older, I needed to find some time for myself.

I deserved it.

Martin

I tried to be cool, but I gave up and texted Lillian the second I got home from the bar. We fell into a pattern. She was radio silent during her working hours, and she refused to respond to texts until I was off work too.

My girl had strong opinions about work time being for work, not personal stuff, and I had to respect that. Plus, it wasn't like she could text me from the factory floor anyway.

Once I confirmed that I was off work for the day, we generally texted a couple of times throughout the evening. Then when the kids were in bed, we'd chat back and forth for hours. It was fun, not as much fun as seeing her in person of course, but it also gave us a way to get to know each other a little better. Our relationship had started with the physical, but I already knew that I wanted to spend the rest of my life with her, whether she realized it yet or not.

By the time our date night came, I was a jumble of nerves. We'd agreed to meet for an early dinner in a good-sized town midway between our houses. I suggested a nice restaurant I'd been to a few times for business, but Lillian vetoed it once she saw their website.

"I'm not a fancy girl," she texted. *"Can't we go somewhere where I don't have to dress up? Despite New Year's Eve, that's not really me."*

"I was trying to impress you," I texted back.

"Don't be an asshole and you'll already be better than most of the guys I dated."

It was a low bar.

We settled on a brew pub that was supposed to have pretty good food in addition to a wide variety of microbrews. Lillian texted that she was running late so I got a table and waited for her inside. She came rushing in, looking the slightest bit harried. She'd worn her hair down today, falling in a curtain down her shoulders. She didn't appear to be wearing make-up other than mascara and lip gloss, but then again, she certainly didn't need it. Her natural beauty was more than enough.

Lillian was wearing dark jeans that hugged her long, muscled legs, black ankle boots with a low heel, and a cute white top with a white tank beneath it.

I pulled her into a hug, sniffing the scent of her shampoo like some kind of a weirdo, and whispered, "I want to fuck you right here."

She pulled back with a laugh. "You're funny."

If she only knew.

We ordered a flight of beer samples, and then a second one as we talked, ate burgers, and shared an enormous basket of tater tots. Lillian was an equal opportunity potato fan.

"This is kind of weird," she confessed midway through the meal. "I'm not a person who goes on dates like this."

I nodded. "Dating is hard with kids. I haven't done a lot of it, to be honest."

"My boys seemed confused when I told them I had a date. It was like I was speaking a foreign language."

"Mine were only interested in the fact that Maria promised to order them pizza and play X-box with them."

We both laughed, then our eyes met and held for a long moment, and the playfulness dissipated. I stared at her, a highlight reel of our New Year's Eve activities rolling through my head. Dancing. Sharing a drink. Dancing again. Making out in the corner as the countdown started. Pulling apart right at midnight intending to say, "Happy New Year's" but instead saying "Come home with me." I didn't remember the drive back to my house, but everything that happened afterward was etched into my brain. I replayed it every day in the shower.

"I want you, Lillian," I whispered.

"I want you too." That was one of the things I loved about Lillian. She was a straight talker. She didn't play games, didn't beat around the bush.

I looked around frantically. "Where can we go?"

Lillian laughed. "We're a little too old to be havin' sex in the bathroom at a restaurant."

"I wasn't even thinking about that," I said in mock outrage. "I thought maybe there was a supply closet some place."

"I can't believe I'm saying this, but isn't there a hotel across the road?"

My cock twitched at the suggestion. It was already half hard and had been since we sat down.

"I don't want you to feel cheap," I said, although I was one hundred percent on board with this hotel idea. It would be way more comfortable than a broom closet.

Lillian leaned forward across the table and gestured for me to do the same. Her face looked incredibly serious, but her eyes twinkled with amusement.

"Martin, I want to tell you a little secret."

"Okay." I leaned closer.

"I've damn near worn out my vibrator the last few weeks fantasizing about what we did on New Year's Eve. I'm kid-free for a few hours, out of batteries, and I'm wearing new panties."

I waved at a passing waitress with both arms, like I was one of those guys directing a plane at the airport.

"Miss? We'd like the check please. Now."

Lillian

I pulled into the parking lot next to Martin's car as I disconnected my call with Luke. He'd assured me that the three of them were watching movies and would be just fine if I came home late.

If my sons were troubled by my sudden interest in dating, Luke didn't mention anything. I hadn't told them that I was going on a date, not at first. I'd only told them I was going out with a friend. They'd taken one look at my new outfit, my blown out hair, and my make-up and quickly figured it out, probably because they knew I didn't dress like that to go for a drink with my buddies at LJ's.

"Are you goin' on a date or somethin' Mama?" Lincoln asked.

"Yeah, I am," I admitted a little sheepishly.

I was surprised when they just nodded and told me to have fun. I'd expected a bunch of questions about who I was dating and where I was going. Of course, that might have taken too much time away from the car chase movie they were watching.

"How long do we have before you have to get home?" Martin asked as we walked hand in hand towards the lobby.

"A few hours."

"Everything's okay at home then?"

"Yeah," I answered. "Luke said everything was quiet."

"My sister said everything is fine on their end too."

We asked the clerk for a room and after a brief tussle over payment, Martin put it on his credit card. The second the elevator door closed he was on me, pressing me into the wall, rolling his hips against mine, and kissing me until the ding of the bell alerted us to our arrival on the fourth floor.

We damn near ran down the hallway.

"Did he put us in the farthest room possible?" I huffed as we finally found our room.

"The clerk was a total cockblocker. He was eyeing you up for himself."

I tapped his arm playfully. "He was not."

Martin looked over his shoulder at me. "You have no idea how gorgeous you are, do you?"

No one had called me gorgeous for a long time, if ever. I knew I wasn't a hag or something. I ate well, other than my love affair with fried potatoes that is. Thanks to my physical job and running around with my boys I was in good shape, avoiding the middle aged spread that was showing up on many of my peers. But it was also pretty rare for me to put even this much effort into my appearance. I didn't need mascara to run parts through a machine or skinny jeans to pick up my kids from a school event.

"You're not that bad lookin' yourself," I teased as he finally got the door open.

"That's the ringing endorsement I was hoping for," he mumbled as we practically fell into the room.

"How's this for an endorsement?"

I pulled my blouse over my head without unbuttoning it, then tugged off my tank top, leaving me in a white lacey bra that I'd spent way too much for when I went to the mall the other day after work.

"This is my new underwear," I said, summoning up what I hoped was a sexy voice.

Martin stared at me with heat in his eyes as I dropped my new jeans to show him the matching panties. Most of my underwear was cotton and utilitarian, but these were a damn work of art.

"How much would you hurt me if I ripped those off you with my teeth?"

And just like that, my brand new panties were soaked.

"Well, I did spend a lot on them."

"You better get them off then," he growled.

He took his own advice and took off his clothes. The instant we were both naked Martin backed me up against the door, pressed his naked body up tight against me, and kissed the stuffing out of me.

"Fuck," I whispered when we finally came up for air. Martin was nipping along my neck and the top of my shoulder while my hands squeezed the firm muscles of his ass.

"Should I get a condom?" he asked.

We'd had this discussion on New Year's Eve. I'd told him I had an IUD and hadn't had a partner in a while, and he'd said it had been a long time for him too. Maybe it had been risky to not use protection that night, but I'd trusted him instinctively. Him reconfirming that it was okay to go in bareback only increased that trust.

"We're good without one."

Martin grabbed the tops of my thighs and boosted me up against the door.

"We got a bed just over there," I reminded him, even as I wrapped my legs around his hips and rolled my pelvis until the tip of his dick slid right between my folds.

"The bed's too far away, I need you now."

He shoved his penis into me so hard I lost my ability to breathe.

"Relax," he whispered against my neck. "You're strangling my cock."

I huffed out a laugh, which helped my internal muscles adjust from the stinging pain of his invasion, leaving behind nothing but pure pleasure. I loved feeling this full with him.

"You good?" he asked.

"Yeah, you can move now." I rolled my hips against him for emphasis.

Martin set a fast pace, slamming me against the door with each hard thrust. He thoughtfully wrapped one hand around the back of my head to shield me from a concussion, and I arched my back to get leverage to meet his strokes.

"You feel so good, Lillian, I...it's never been like this before."

He pulled back to look at me, to let me see the truth in his eyes.

"I know, me neither."

Martin

Lillian's words spurred me on, and I redoubled my efforts, sliding upwards against her with every stroke so my pubic bone ground against her clitoris. She was getting close, I could tell by the fluttering of her pussy.

I was desperate to mark her as mine, and just painting her womb with my cum wasn't going to be enough, I could tell already, so I lowered my head, sunk my teeth into the juncture of her neck, and sucked hard.

It was such a primal urge, this urge to let the world know that Lillian was mine, but as soon as I sucked her flesh into my mouth she came with a wail. She shuddered between me and the door, my name on her lips, and when I lifted my head, her face was the very picture of ecstasy.

The sight of it made my balls draw up and I spurted my cum inside with several hard thrusts of my hips. When I'd finally emptied myself, I lowered my head to her neck again, kissing the rather impressive mark I'd left there, while we caught our breath.

"Holy shit."

It was the same thing she'd said the first time we had sex. It made me feel kind of proud of myself.

I stepped back, carrying her to the bed with our bodies still attached, her hands clutching my shoulders. I sat on the bed, and Lillian straddled my lap as I pressed a soft kiss against her lips.

"I thought it was just the fantasy of that night," she said softly. "The fancy dress, the make-up, the dancing...it seemed too good to be true. But it wasn't, was it?"

I shook my head. "If anything, it was better the second time."

"Well, technically this was like our fourth time, maybe fifth, I lost count that night." Her voice was teasing, and I loved this fun side of her.

"I don't know if we'll have enough time to beat that number tonight," I cautioned.

"There's always next time."

I squeezed her tight. "I hope so."

"By the way, did you give me a hickey?"

I gave her a sheepish look. "Maybe?"

"You'd better hope no one sees that, buddy, or we're gonna have words."

"I'd rather have sex."

One month later...

"How are things with Lillian?" Maria asked after the kids went to bed.

"Good."

I paused for just a second too long, and Maria jumped on it. My sister had always been intuitive, and given that she was my best friend, she could tune into my emotions pretty well.

"What? What's wrong?"

I got up and went to the high cabinet over the refrigerator, returning with a bottle of tequila. Maria jumped up to get glasses. We always had our most important discussions over tequila. We'd been close even as kids, but when she moved in to help parent my kids, our relationship had deepened even more.

I poured us each a shot as I considered the best way to answer the question.

"Things are good, but they suck at the same time."

"What do you mean?" Maria took a sip of her tequila. We'd long ago graduated to the expensive kind that was meant for sipping, instead of the cheap stuff you knocked back in one gulp with lime and salt.

"We text all the time—."

"Yeah, I've noticed you're getting text thumb," my sister teased. "You'll probably have to learn how to text with more than two fingers."

My sister did a fair amount of texting with her new boyfriend, but I resisted mentioning that.

"We've only been able to manage a once a week date. We meet in Redmond, have dinner, then go to a hotel for a few hours.

It's…incredible, but it's also starting to feel like we're just each other's booty call."

"Well, big brother, I think it's time for you to step it up."

"Step it up?"

"Meet each other's friends, introduce each other to the kids, that kind of thing." She snapped her fingers. "Oh, I know, we should have a dinner party."

"A dinner party?"

"Yeah, we can sucker mom and dad into taking the kids overnight, then you can invite Lillian and I can invite John. We'll each invite a couple of our friends, then I'll go home with John, and Lillian can sleep over here with you."

John was the new boyfriend. They seemed pretty happy together so far. I liked him way better than that guy Scott she'd been with at the New Year's Eve party.

"I don't know if Lillian's going to be up for a sleepover," I said. "She's been pretty adamant about not leaving her kids home alone."

"I thought they were older than our boys. Didn't you say they were teenagers?"

Maria considered the kids just as much hers as mine and given that she'd been like a mother to them, I didn't disagree.

"They are. The oldest is eighteen, but Lillian doesn't think it sets a good example for them if she's off having sex all night while they're home alone. Plus, I think we all remember what it's like to be an unsupervised teenager. There's a high probability of trouble, even if they're good kids."

"Well, if y'all stay together, sooner or later you're going to have to start sleeping over and figuring out how to incorporate the kids into your relationship," Maria said. "You can't keep everything separate forever. Even little Charlie has noticed that you have a regular playdate every week."

"Playdate?" I laughed.

"Last week Mark asked me if you had a girlfriend," she told me.

Mark was my twelve-year-old.

"I can't believe he didn't ask me."

"Well, all three of them were very curious about why you've been out late so I told them that you had a new best friend and you were going on playdates."

I burst out laughing. "That's one way to describe it."

"Well, Mark is still curious, but it cut off the questions. For now. But at some point, you need to have a talk with them."

Lillian

Martin had a meeting with the bigwigs at Thomas Industries today. He'd purposely scheduled it later in the day so we could get together for a little while afterwards. He wanted to meet me outside the factory, but I wasn't in the mood to deal with a lot of nosy questions from my friends and coworkers, so I suggested we meet at LJ's instead. When I got there Martin had already ordered me a beer and a basket of fries. He was a good man.

"Hey," I said, leaning down to give him a quick peck on the cheek.

He slid out of the booth, wrapping me into his arms for a proper kiss before releasing me. When he tried to slide into the booth next to me I shooed him over to the other side.

"I can't talk to you if I have to turn my head all the damn time," I grumbled, even though I loved the way he wanted to be close to me. "Sit across from me like a regular person."

We'd been seeing each other for almost six weeks now and while it was great, something was missing. I guess I never knew how difficult it would be to date someone who lived in another town and had a schedule as crazy as mine was.

Becky kept insisting that we were keeping each other at a distance on purpose to avoid the inevitable complications of bringing our families into the mix. Maybe she was right. I hadn't dated anyone seriously since my divorce. I had no idea how to be in love and still focus on my kids.

And I was in love too. Whole-heartedly, head over heels, madly in love. Not that I'd told anyone, including Martin. It seemed ridiculous to be this smitten at my age, but as my mother used to tell me, you feel how you feel, and there's no accounting for feelings.

"I think it's time we take the next step."

I looked up in surprise at his words.

"What?" I said, stalling for time. "What next step?"

"Maria and I were thinking about having a dinner party at our house. She finally ditched that tool Scott and is dating this new guy John who seems frighteningly normal. We thought we could invite some of our friends, and then you and John could meet our everybody."

He pinned me with an intense look. "Then afterward, you could spend the night with me."

"Are you asking me to have a sleepover?" I teased.

"I am."

"What about your sister? Isn't her room across the hall from yours?"

"She already said she'd go to her boyfriend's so we could have some privacy."

"And where will your boys be during this hypothetical sleepover?"

"Staying at their grandparents. Maybe yours can do the same?"

I shook my head. "I never ask my parents to help with the boys. Ever."

"Sounds like there's a story there."

"There is. When I divorced my ex-husband, they told me in no uncertain terms that I was an idiot, and a little cheating wasn't something to break up a family for. They tried to convince me to stay with Brad, and when I refused, they said I'd better not ever ask them for anything since I was making a terrible mistake. I've never asked them for a damn thing since then, even when they offer to help, I tell them no."

"Wow, that's...I honestly don't know what to say about that, Lil, other than I'm sorry that happened."

I frowned pensively into my beer, thinking about how betrayed I'd felt by my parents. I rarely spoke to them, and I refused to spend holidays with them. I allowed the boys to have whatever level of relationship they felt comfortable with having, but even though they didn't know why we'd had a falling out, they'd made it clear to my parents that they were on my side.

All three of my brothers had moved away by the time I got divorced, and while I'd always been close with Lewis and his wife Sue, they didn't live close enough for me to call on them for last minute favors.

Thank God I'd had Becky when the boys were younger. She was the one person I could always count on. It broke my heart when she moved away to Houston a few years ago. She'd moved away for a man, and while that didn't last, she'd fallen in love with the city and decided to stay. We still talked every day though.

"Is there anyone else who could keep an eye on things for you?" he asked hopefully.

I shifted through my mental rolodex. The truth was there were a bunch of people who owed me favors. Maybe just this once I could call them in.

"I might could find someone," I said.

Becky would probably come from Houston if I asked, or maybe George and Cassie could hang out with them.

Martin's face broke out in a big smile. "So, you'll come to the party, meet my friends, and then spend the night with me?"

I nodded. "Yeah."

"You know what comes next, don't you?" he asked. "We need to meet each other's kids. And introduce them to each other."

That had the potential to go very badly.

"Let's take one thing at a time, okay?" I suggested.

A few days later Luke knocked on the door to my bedroom where I was holed up texting with Martin like a smitten teenager.

"You got a minute, Mama?"

"Of course," I said, waving him in and dropping my phone into the drawer of my nightstand.

Luke sat on the other end of the bed and gave me a long look. He was looking so grown up, more like a man than the boy he used to be. It made my heart ache.

"Is it getting' serious?"

"What?"

"You and this guy you've been seeing for the last couple of months," he paused, then added, "Or woman. I mean, it's okay if it's a woman you're seeing."

I rolled my lips in to keep myself from laughing. "It's a guy," I said. "His name is Martin."

Luke nodded. It was the first time any of the boys had asked about my date nights, and frankly I was surprised it had taken so long.

"We haven't been askin' you anything about this guy," Luke continued, as if he heard my thoughts. "We didn't want you to feel uncomfortable or something by violating your privacy. You're always tellin' us that you're entitled to privacy the same as us."

Well, that was a surprise.

"But me and the boys were talkin' and if y'all are getting serious, we're gonna need to meet him. Make sure he's good enough for our Mama."

He looked so serious right now I couldn't stand it. "Oh, I see."

"You know I'm goin' away to college in a few months, and it won't be long before Linc and Logan are all grown up too."

I resisted pointing out that at eighteen he wasn't as grown up as he thought. Then again, Luke had always been mature for his age, wise beyond his years. He'd been the most hurt when his father left.

"I know you gave up a lot to take care of us, Mama," Luke continued. "But we don't want you to be alone forever. It's not healthy for a woman to be alone."

"It's not healthy for anyone to be alone," I corrected. "And I'm not alone, I've got you boys."

Luke stood up, giving me what I'm sure he thought was a stern look. "We want to meet this guy. Soon."

Martin

"I had an interesting conversation with Luke the other day."

Our dinner party was a rousing success. My friends all loved Lillian and she seemed to like them too. She'd insisted on coming early to help set up, which earned her brownie points with Maria. The two of them had spent the rest of the night ganging up on me and laughing over every embarrassing story Maria could dredge up about me.

It made me happy that they got along so well.

Once everyone left, I'd grabbed a bottle of wine and two glasses and dragged Lillian up to my room. The first time we made love it was fast and rough, but the second time was slow and sweet, much more relaxed than we'd ever been before. It helped that we weren't on a time limit like we usually had when we were at the hotel.

There was something to be said about being able to take your time.

"What did you and Luke talk about?" I asked.

"The boys have decided that if I'm getting serious about a fella, they need to meet him to make sure he's good enough for me."

"That makes sense," I said. "I'd feel the same way if my mama was dating some guy."

"Maria told me that your boys have been asking about you going out too and whether you had a girlfriend, which made me think you're right. It's probably about time for us to meet each other's kids."

I was thrilled at this conversation. She didn't realize it yet, but I wanted to spend the rest of my life with Lillian. But we couldn't move in that direction until we started doing more than having quickies at the Hotel Six.

"What's our plan of attack?" I asked. "Divide and conquer? Or bring them all together at once and let the chips fall where they may?"

"Well, that's a good question. I'm kinda thinking we plan some kind of group activity where we can take the pressure off a bit."

"Like paintball?"

"Oh God no, my boys will kill you dead if they got weapons in their hands. We all take our paintball very seriously."

I could totally see that, just based on what I knew about Lillian. My woman was tough and super competitive.

"Oh I got it, what about if we have dinner at Dave and Buster's in Houston? Once we get the awkward conversation out of the way, we can eat wings and burgers and then I can kick your ass at pinball."

Lillian rose up on one elbow, one eyebrow raised. "You think you can beat me, buddy? Those are fighting words. I think you're the one who's gonna get the ass kickin.'"

"Shall we place a friendly wager?" I teased.

"What do you have in mind?"

I whispered my idea in her ear, and she burst out laughing. "I had no idea you were such a kinky bastard."

I rolled her over, pinning her to the mattress with my hips. I grabbed my pants off the floor and slid my belt out of the loops, using it to tie her hands to the headboard while she pretended to struggle. By the time I was done we were both laughing.

"Well, now that you got me here, what are you going to do now?" she asked.

"I'm going to kiss my way down your body and lick your sweet pussy until you come all over my face."

"I approve of this plan."

We'd already had sex twice and between that and my teasing her, Lillian was soaking wet. I loved it. I gripped her thighs in my hands and licked up and down her opening until she was thrashing beneath me. Between having her hands tied above her head and my hands immobilizing her legs, she was pretty much at my mercy.

I'd learned early on that Lillian didn't like to be treated like a delicate flower. She liked her sex hard and rough, and I did too, but it didn't need to be that way every time we were together. As she began to trust me more, she was able to relax enough for us to mix it up and spend more time leisurely exploring each other's bodies too.

Since we had all night, I took my time, bringing her close to orgasm again and again until she was swearing up a blue streak and threatening to castrate me with just her fingers when she was free again. I gave her a big smile from between her legs, then bit down on her clit, sending her right over the edge.

Lillian screamed so loud I was surprised the neighbors didn't come over to see what was going on.

When she finally came down from her orgasm, I kissed my way back up her body until I was laying on top of her. Propping myself up on my elbows, I stared down at her for a long moment before I said what I'd been waiting to say since the night I met her.

"I need to tell you that I love you, Lillian. I've loved you for a long time."

A range of emotions crossed her face. I didn't know what I was expecting her to say, but "Untie my hands" would not have been my first guess. Terrified that I'd made a mistake sharing my feelings, I rolled off of her and freed her hands, taking a moment to rub both of her wrists with my fingers.

She popped up to a sitting position, watching me carefully.

"You love me?" she finally asked.

"Yeah, I do." Still unsure what she was thinking, I did my best to convey all my emotions in my expression.

"Hm."

After a painfully long pause she added, "I thought I was in love once, but I was wrong. Please don't make me be wrong again, Martin."

"Are you saying...?"

"Yeah, I'm sayin' that I love you, Martin. I'm not sure if or how this is gonna work out between us, but I love you enough to commit to figuring it out."

I pulled her into my arms, pressing her head against my chest, and kissed the top of her hair.

"I can't believe you told me you love me."

She sighed, but I could sense that she was smiling. "Yeah, yeah, just don't let it go to your head."

Lillian

When I sat down at the table in the lunchroom, all eyes turned to me.

"Well?"

I spared Jimmy a quick glance before returning my attention the Tupperware lid that seemed to be stuck on the container.

"Well, what?"

I knew exactly what he was asking, but messing with Jimmy was one of my favorite activities.

"How'd it go introducing your boys to Martin and his kids?" he asked impatiently.

"Josie was begging' me and David for us to all go over to Dave and Buster's so we could 'casually' run into you," George shared, making air quotes around the word casually.

George's sister Josie was easily the nosiest person in this entire town, although she was also one of the nicest, which helped.

"Cassandra got her to calm down though," George added.

Cassandra was George's fiancée. We'd all met her when she came to Thomas Industries to study our production line for efficiency challenges. We'd all been a little suspicious of her, like we were of anyone from corporate, but it turned out she knew her stuff. With Cassie's help we'd made some improvements to our processes and kept the suits in the corporate office from deciding to outsource our work to Mexico.

Thank God, because there was hardly anywhere else to work in this town, so we all would have been in serious trouble without the factory.

George's brother-in-law, David, had asked him to work with Cassandra, playing the family card to get cooperation. The two of them didn't like each other at first, but as George and Cassie worked together, they fell in love. They were a perfect match.

Cassie wound up finding a job in Houston that was mostly remote and then she moved in with George and his geriatric basset hound, Bart.

The three of them were adorable together and we were all hoping George would nut up soon and officially propose to her.

"I'm glad Cassie has some respect for people's privacy at least," I said, taking a bite of my sandwich.

"Come on, Lillian. Tell us everything," Leo wheedled.

I decided to take pity on them.

"You know what? It mostly went fine. We got there a little bit late because Lincoln is in his forty-minute shower stage..."

Jimmy guffawed. "It's not about the shower."

I sighed deeply with exaggerated patience. "Yes Jimmy, I know. Thank you so much for pointing out that my sixteen year old son, the same boy who was sleeping with a teddy bear until he was eleven and used to cry every day when I went to work because he didn't want to be away from his Mama, now needs to use most of the hot water in the house so he can jack off."

"So you were a little late...," Leo prompted, redirecting my attention from Jimmy.

"Yeah so, we sit down at one of those long tables, Martin's family on one side and mine on the other, and there's this awkward silence after the introductions while everyone is sizing each other up. Then Luke puffs himself up, gives Martin his best glare, the one he uses to strike fear in the minds of every opponent he meets on the football field, and he tells Martin that he'd like to know what Martin's intentions are towards me."

Everyone at the table laughed.

"How did Martin handle that?" Leo asked.

"Well, he looked Luke in the eye man to man and said that he loved me and hoped that someday, after we'd been dating for an appropriate amount of time, that I'd agree to marry him. My boys were all in shock, but his boys were super chill about it. Martin told me later that his youngest had asked in the car on the way over if we were getting married and Martin had basically already told them the same thing, so it wasn't a surprise when he said it to Luke."

"Y'all have talked about getting' married?" George asked. "Already?"

He was one to talk. He and Cassie had moved in together within two months of meeting each other.

I shook my head emphatically. "No sir, we have not talked about any such thing. I would have been annoyed about him talking to the kids about it before me if it wasn't so damned sweet."

"You weren't annoyed because you do want to marry that boy," Leo pointed out. "We ain't never seen you excited about someone like this before, Lillian, including when that useless ex-husband of yours came a' courtin'."

I couldn't argue with that, so I didn't.

"What happened after that?" Jimmy asked.

"Luke and Linc just nodded like the matter was settled, but Logan asked if we got married were the other boys gonna be his brothers. Mark – that's Martin's oldest – said yes that's how it works when parents get married. Logan said he hoped we did get married then, because he is sick of being the youngest and he wouldn't mind having some little brothers."

I shook my head at boy logic. "Then they ate about a hundred pounds of hot wings and several burgers each and ran off to play games in the arcade. All the boys bonded with each other over games."

"Did you and Martin have a talk after that?"

"Oh hell no, I dragged him over to the closest pin ball machine and kicked his ass, then I beat him in Space Invaders too just to make my point."

"It's important to show dominance in a relationship," Jimmy said.

"What the hell do you know about a relationship, boy?" Leo asked. "You ain't dated hardly at all the entire time I've known you."

Jimmy got a sappy look on his face. "Yeah, but some day I'm gonna find love, just like you had with Anna, and like these two have now too." He gestured towards me and George.

Leo clapped him on the back, his eyes misty at the mention of his deceased wife. "I hope so, for your sake. Love is the best thing in the world."

Martin

Things had been going pretty smoothly the last two months. Now that Lillian and I had met each other's kids, we felt a little more comfortable seeing each other when they were around. After our successful lunch and video game trip to Dave and Buster's, the eight of us went to the movies one Saturday. We took up an entire row, and spent a small fortune on popcorn and snacks, but everyone seemed to have fun. We'd also all had dinner together twice now.

We hadn't done any sleepovers while the kids were around – in fact, we'd only done two sleepovers since that first one at my house – but that was going to change today. Lillian's friend George had finally proposed to his girlfriend, and George's sister was having a big engagement party for the couple. Because it would run late and likely involve alcohol, Lillian suggested I sleep over at her house afterwards.

I was thrilled, both by Lillian wanting to take me to an event with all her friends, and by the idea that she was allowing me into her home. It felt like a big step. The party was happening on a Saturday, so after spending the day with my own kids, I left them in Maria's care and headed towards Lillian's place.

As I drove there, I thought about the bomb my sister had dropped on me last night: her boyfriend wanted them to move in together. They were in love, but she wasn't sure if she was ready to take that step. I had a feeling that part of her reluctance was her feeling obligated to help me. But the fact was, the boys were older now, and with them being more self-sufficient, it gave both me and my sister more time to have personal lives.

Lillian lived in a large ranch house on a corner lot. I hadn't been there before, but I was unsurprised to find the property tidy, with neatly cut grass and two large flower gardens on either side of the porch, a rocking swing hanging from chains on one side. I imagined Lillian sitting on the swing drinking coffee and getting a bit of peace and quiet before she had to go to work.

One thing I'd learned about Lillian was that she was always in motion. Other than when I'd worn her out with enough orgasms for her to sleep, she was always fidgeting or cleaning something with a cloth or straightening pictures, even when she was visiting my place. But early morning was her quiet time, she'd told me.

Logan, her youngest boy, answered the door when I knocked.

"Hey, Martin." He greeted me with all the enthusiasm a fourteen-year-old boy could muster. "Mom's in here."

Lillian was on the couch, locked in what looked like X-box death match with Lincoln. They were both leaning forward on the couch, eyes glued to the screen, their faces masks of concentration as they punched at the controller.

"Hi everyone."

Lillian made a noise that might have been a greeting.

"She's trying to finally beat Linc," Luke told me from the recliner. "Don't interrupt her concentration or she'll kill you."

I sat in the other chair, watching with amusement until the game was finally over. Lillian jumped up, punching her fist in the air.

"I did it! Ha! I did it! I beat Lincoln!"

"Mama, what's that you always tell us about being graceful winners?" Luke asked in mock disapproval.

She stuck her tongue out at him, then walked over to me, giving me a quick peck on the cheek. I snaked my arms around her as she moved away, pulling her in for a hug. She wrapped her arms around my waist and rested her cheek on my chest with a sigh.

One of the boys made a gagging noise and she pulled away with an eye roll.

"I just need a few minutes to get ready for the party. Do you want to join me?"

"Maybe later," I said, noting that the boys were watching me carefully. It was one thing to sleep over, another thing to have them thinking we were doing something while they were awake and hanging out in the living room.

While Lillian was getting ready, I watched a basketball game on TV with her boys. They didn't talk much, but with three boys at home I was used to their lack of communication skills.

Lillian returned twenty minutes later wearing an outfit I'd never seen before. I suspected it was new.

She was wearing a white sundress printed with tiny yellow daisies. The top part was fitted, then it flared out over her hips and thighs. She'd paired it with a short denim jacket and a pair of black cowboy boots. With her long hair brushed out and down around her shoulders and a touch of dark pink gloss on her lips, she looked like the Texas girl next door.

I wanted to push her against the wall and have my way with her but given that her three sons were in the room, I cleared my throat and said, "You look real nice."

She gave me a small smile. "Thanks."

"Wow, Mama, you look really pretty, like a girl."

I could see her debating about how to respond to Logan's heartfelt compliment, but in the end, she just gave him a smile.

Turning to pin the three of them with a 'mom' look she said, "Okay, listen up. I ordered the pizzas and prepaid for them. It should be here within half an hour. There's coke and orange juice in the fridge but no more than one sugary drink each, and you have to drink at least one bottle of water each with dinner too. Got it?"

"Yes, Mama," they chorused.

"And don't you dare eat all the cookies or we will be havin' an unpleasant conversation tomorrow."

"Yes, Mama."

"Me and Martin are gonna be at Josie and David's house and that's only eight blocks away. Call me on my cell phone but only if it's an emergency, like one of you have a broken bone protruding through your skin or the house is on fire."

She paused, then added, "Oh yeah, please don't set the house on fire."

"We'll be fine, we're old enough to stay home alone for a few hours without gettin' in trouble," Logan said, exasperation thick in his voice. "Luke is a legal adult, you know."

Lillian reached over and ruffled his hair, causing him to roll his eyes in a way that only teenagers could do.

"Y'all are still my babies, no matter what the state of Texas says."

She held out her hand to me and gave me a big smile. "C'mon sexy, it's time to go party."

Behind us a trio of groans sounded.

Lillian

Dancing with Martin brought me back to our first night together. Tonight, like then, I was wearing a dress and make-up, but this was nowhere near the fancy dress and sophisticated make-up that I'd worn that night. It didn't matter though. Martin seemed to like me just fine when I was in my regular day-to-day outfit of faded jeans, tee shirts, a sports bra, and work boots.

It was nice, dressing up and going to a party on the arm of a handsome man who professed to love me.

Even though I hadn't dated that much since my divorce, I'd convinced myself that no one would want a single mother with three boys in their life. And the act of dating itself seemed selfish when I was trying to keep food on the table and make sure my kids were raised right.

But this thing, whatever it was that I had with Martin, felt good. Comfortable. I just wasn't sure how long it could last. Between us we had six kids, two full-time jobs, two houses, and a 'to do' list a mile long. It didn't leave very much time for us to have grown up time, especially with us living thirty minutes away from each other – forty-five when the traffic was bad. And the traffic was only bad on days that ended with a Y.

As I watched George and Cassie make the rounds at their party, accepting congratulations from their friends and family, I felt a twinge of envy. It wasn't like me – I was usually a very practical and stoic person – but it was there nonetheless. I wouldn't mind a party like this for me and Martin someday – if we could ever figure out how to be together more than a few times a month that is.

When we got home after the party, tipsy and happy, the house was quiet. After popping my head in and verifying that the boys were all asleep, we headed downstairs.

I'd converted most of the basement into a master suite with a large bedroom, sitting room, and bathroom. It was warm and comfortable, my sanctuary away from noisy boys having belching contests or playing video games. A place completely absent of foul-smelling sweat socks on the floor, toothpaste detritus in the sink, or toilet seats in the wrong position.

The minute I closed the door I was on Martin, kissing him and practically tearing off his clothes. We made love twice before falling asleep in each other's arms. It was only the fourth time we'd been able to spend the whole night with each other, fifth if you counted New Year's Eve, and my last thought before I drifted to sleep was that I wished I could do this every single night.

I woke up when Martin got out of bed the next morning.

"Where are you going?" I mumbled.

"I have to use the bathroom, then I thought I'd go upstairs and make us some coffee." He paused, probably thinking he sounded too presumptuous. "I mean, if it's okay to make coffee? We could drink it in bed."

I knew that wasn't the only thing he wanted to do in bed this morning. I could see his morning wood clear as day, so he was probably going to have to wait a bit before he could pee.

"You bring me coffee in bed, and I'll love you forever," I teased.

I snuggled back under the blankets, almost falling asleep again before I heard the door open and Martin called down, "Lillian? Honey? I think you'd better get up here."

I popped right out of bed and was pulling on a robe and heading for the stairs before I even thought about it. After years of being a single mother I was highly attuned to panicked voices, and Martin definitely had a tone of panic in his voice.

When I got upstairs Martin was leaning against the counter looking uncomfortable while my parents glared at him from the middle of the room. Martin was wearing a pair of sleep pants and nothing else, his rumpled hair making him look extra adorable.

"Mama? Daddy? What are y'all doing here at this hour?"

My relationship with my parents had been strained since the divorce and if it wasn't for the boys, I likely wouldn't talk to them at all. They'd made their choice during the divorce, and it wasn't their daughter. That was one thing I couldn't forgive. One thing that *they* couldn't forgive is that I hadn't needed them to bail me out once since the day I kicked my ex-husband to the curb.

"This hour?" My mother's voice was dripping with disdain. "It's nine a.m."

The coffee pot sputtered to a stop and Martin poured two cups of coffee, handing one to me. He stood close in a show of solidarity, his arm around my waist, while drinking his coffee with his other hand.

"I don't need to justify my sleeping' habits to you Mama. So, I'll ask you again – what are you doing here barging into my house without an invitation?"

"Mabel Parker called me to say that there was a strange car in your driveway overnight, so of course we came right over to see if you were being held hostage or something."

My mother's eyes cut to Martin, her expression clearly indicating that she still wasn't sure about the hostage thing.

"We knocked and knocked and when no one answered, well, we used the emergency key to come in," my mother answered.

Despite living in the same town, I hadn't seen my parents in at least six weeks, and that had just been in passing at the Kroger grocery store. My mother had pretended not to see me.

I couldn't decide if they were here to assuage their curiosity or if they just wanted to look like good grandparents in front of Mabel. God knows they cared more about their reputation in town than they did about their daughter and grandkids.

"No one answered because everyone here is sleeping," I said firmly. "Y'all are gonna need to leave now. Don't you ever come in here like that again. And give me my keys back before you let yourselves out."

Just then the boys came into the kitchen, no doubt wondering what all the ruckus was. My mother's eyes swung from the boys to me and Martin and back to the boys, her face turning redder by the minute. My father stood silently as usual, serving as her sentry.

"Lillian Antonia Wainwright! I raised you better than to expose your impressionable young sons to this kind of filth. They don't need to see their mama canoodling with a half-naked man and acting like a common slut!"

"Hey!" Luke and Martin bellowed simultaneously.

"I don't care who you are, lady, you don't get to talk to her like that," Martin said firmly.

"Yeah, you are way outta line, Grandma," Luke added belligerently.

Lincoln and Logan moved closer, closing ranks on us and sending my mother their own angry glares. One thing about my boys, they were as protective of me as I was of them.

My mother rested her hand on her chest like she was fixing to have a heart attack from all the stress. "Well, I just can't believe this behavior…"

"Cut the drama queen act, Mama. This is the first time you've stepped foot in this house or shown any interest in me in years. You stopped being able to tell me how to live my life the moment you decided to choose a lying cheating asshole over your own daughter. You satisfied your curiosity about who was visiting me, y'all can go on home now."

"How dare you talk about Brad like that in front of his boys? You need to show some respect for their father!"

"Daddy didn't show no respect for Mama, and he certainly ain't shown any interest in us," Luke said firmly. "Now I believe my mama asked you to leave."

With one last glare at me, my mother stormed out, my father close on her heels. The man hadn't said a word the entire time they were there. After they left, we all stood in stunned silence for a full minute.

"Well, that was weird," Lincoln finally said, his tone dry.

"Yes, it was," I agreed. "I'm going to need some waffles and bacon after all that. Who's up for breakfast at Main Street Diner?"

Martin

If there was one thing that brought men together, it was standing up for women. Any reserve that Lillian's sons had toward me melted, and the three of them talked and laughed with me as we all walked the short way over to the diner where we were having breakfast.

I saw a couple of people look at us curiously, their eyes fixed on my fingers twined around Lillian's, but no one bothered us as we settled at one of the larger tables and had a delicious breakfast.

I'd had a great night with Lillian. I'd enjoyed meeting her friends, enjoyed dancing with her again, and most of all I'd enjoyed waking up next to her this morning, something we rarely got to do. But even after several months of dating, I just wasn't sure how we would ever blend our lives.

Our distance was the elephant in the room. It would be easier if we all lived in the same town, but the idea of asking either set of kids to leave their schools and their friends so that Lillian and I could be together seemed incredibly unfair.

The next several weeks were particularly difficult. We were deep into spring and all six of the kids had activities most days. Add in that Lillian's factory was on mandatory overtime, and I had several business trips across the state, and we managed to go more than a month without seeing each other in person.

It all came to a head one night on a video call.

Lillian and I both had our phones out, thumbing through calendars looking for days we could spare a few hours, but any day we chose didn't work. It was an exercise in futility that we'd been going through over and over for weeks.

"How about dinner Wednesday after next?" I suggested.

Lillian shook her head. "We're still on mandatory OT, I'll be doing double shifts all month. I'm dead on my feet after a sixteen-hour day."

"Sunday the fourteenth?"

"No, Logan has a baseball game."

On and on it went with us, unable to find anything that worked.

"I guess I could come by for a quick visit on Thursday when you get off at eight," I said glumly. "But I'd need to head right back after, I have an early meeting the next day."

Lillian set her phone down and peered at the screen, her face serious. My stomach sank.

"I love you, Martin, but I gotta be honest. This really isn't working out for us, and we both know it. We can't have a relationship that consists of only text messages and the occasional video call."

My heart stuttered in my chest, even though I knew she was right. "We just need to try harder. Maybe Maria can attend—."

She held up her palm.

"No, she's got her own relationship now and you do not want to be that dad who misses his kid's games, same as I don't want to miss any of my kids' stuff. Face it, we each have three very busy kids, and our lives are stressful enough without us putting extra pressure on ourselves trying to fit our relationship into the tiny little slivers of time we can find. This is crazy making, Martin."

I nodded sadly. "I want nothing more than for us to go to bed together every night and wake up together every morning," I said, a catch in my voice.

"I want that too, but my life is not about me, just like your life is not about you. Face it, we live too far away, and things are way too complicated with all these kids. I'm afraid it's just not our time to be together."

"Can we still talk? Be friends?"

She blinked rapidly like she was trying not to cry.

"I'll always love you Martin, but it's probably best if we make a clean break."

Lillian

Four weeks later...

"You're comin' to LJ's with us, right Miss Lillian?"

"Not tonight, Jimmy," I threw the response over my shoulder without even looking at him. "Thanks anyway."

A shadow blocked out the light as George moved in front of me. The guy was gentle as a kitten but tall and wide like a mountain. His expression was stony.

"You're coming with us," he said firmly. "You need to get out. You've spent enough time wallowing."

I blinked at his tone. Usually, I was the one ordering people around while George was watching in amusement.

"I'm not wallowing," I protested weakly.

I was totally wallowing. For a guy I hadn't spent a lot of time with, Martin was surprisingly hard to get over. I missed him every minute of every day. I missed texting with him. I missed our video calls. I really missed having sex with him. Most of all, I missed having someone who loved me.

"Good, then you can join us at LJ's for a beer and some conversation," Leo said, coming up on my other side and linking his arm with mine.

"I guess I'm going for a drink," I muttered.

I was half tempted to ditch them once I got to my car, but I knew my friends well enough to know that they'd just show up at my house if I didn't come with them. We were an odd little group of besties: strong and silent George, grizzled old-timer Leo, young jokester Jimmy, and den mother Lillian, but it worked for us. We had other friends at work of course, but the four of us were more like family.

After calling Luke to let the boys know that I'd be late, I drove the short distance to the bar. I hadn't been here since the last time I'd snuck in some time with Martin, and just thinking about him made my heart pinch. Would it ever get easier?

I knew I'd done the right thing breaking up with him, despite my strong feelings for him. We'd spent so much time wrangling schedules and driving back and forth and organizing our lives around our kids, we simply didn't have time for a relationship. But that didn't mean I didn't spend a lot of time wishing it was different.

My best friend had a lot of opinions on the matter. Becky was convinced that after us each getting ditched by our spouses, Martin and I were using schedules and distances as an excuse to avoid real intimacy. She didn't buy the argument that we couldn't move closer and blend our lives any more than she believed that our kids would be the barrier we thought it was.

Of course, if it was up to Becky, I'd be living some Brady Bunch life, only I didn't think we'd be able to find a live-in housekeeper willing to put up with six boys. Not that we could afford to hire an Alice anyway. Martin and I both made good salaries, but not live-in help salaries, especially when we had so many boys to feed.

I waved a greeting to Chrissy who was working behind the bar, then looked around for my friends. Even though they'd all left before me, I didn't see any of them in the bar.

"They guys are waitin' for you in the back room, Lillian," Chrissy called.

Now that was weird. The back room at LJ's was where you went for bachelor parties and wedding rehearsals, not a quick drink with your work buddies after shift. It wasn't like the main part of the bar was that busy tonight, there were plenty of tables open.

When I opened the door to the party room I reared back in shock. In addition to Leo, George, and Jimmy, there were other familiar faces gathered around the table. Luke, Lincoln, and Logan sat next to Becky, all of them looking super serious.

"What is this?" I joked. "An intervention?"

Becky hopped up and pulled me down into a chair, putting her arm around me. "That's exactly what this is, sweetie. An intervention."

I looked around the table in confusion.

"You idiots know I don't do drugs, right? And I haven't had a drink in weeks."

I hadn't touched alcohol since my last date with Martin. I'd wanted to drink several times since the break-up, but I'd resisted it, knowing that if I started, I wouldn't be able to stop until I'd numbed the pain of my broken heart.

"Who wants to start?" Leo asked.

I sent him a surprised look. The only person who liked talking about feelings and personal shit less than Leo was…

"I'll start," George volunteered.

I reached across the table and grabbed an empty glass, filling it with beer from the pitcher on the table. I had a feeling I was going to need that drink now. Too bad they hadn't ordered any fries to go with it.

"Lillian, you know we all like you a lot…," George started.

"We love you, Mama," Logan interjected. My youngest was incredibly sweet and affectionate, something that I hoped he didn't lose as he progressed into his teen years.

George nodded. "That's right, we all love you. That's why we've all brought you here so we can talk about your broken heart."

"Wait, this little intervention is about Martin?" I asked in surprise.

I couldn't decide how I felt about that. Maybe talking about drinking would have been an easier subject. Or my secret obsession with Oreo cookies, one of the only things I'd felt like eating since Martin and I broke up.

"Yes. We've been worried about you. You look terrible, like you're not eating or sleeping."

"I eat," I said defensively.

I hadn't had much of an appetite since the break-up, but it wasn't like I was wasting away. Cookies counted as eating, right? As for sleeping, it was suddenly harder to sleep alone than it had been for all those years before I spent a few nights with Martin.

"Ever since you dumped him, you've been a bear at work," Jimmy added. "I ain't never seen you so cranky before, Miss Lillian. Even the foreman is afraid to talk to you now."

I sighed deeply, tamping down my irritation. I knew it all came from a place of love. Besides, if the foreman was afraid of me now, I really didn't mind that much. I'm sure he thought I was just having a really long menstrual period.

"I appreciate your concern, everyone, but I'm fine, really."

"Mama, don't you know how an intervention goes?" Logan asked impatiently. "We all gotta say something first before you talk. Then you gotta promise to change. I've seen it on TV before."

I took another sip of my beer and leaned back in my seat. "I'm sorry for messing up the intervention, Logan. By all means, go right ahead."

"I was really likin' the idea of being a big brother, and we had fun when we all went out together," Logan said. "You know that we been talking to those guys, right? We didn't break up with them when you broke up with their daddy."

"You're still talking to Martin's boys?" I asked in surprise.

"Yep, and they are havin' an intervention of their own at this very minute."

My eyes flew to my youngest. "Why?"

"Cuz those guys are havin' the same problem with their daddy as we're having with you, Mama."

"Martin is a good guy, Mama," Luke inserted. "He treated you like a lady and defended you to Grandma."

"I know honey, but it's complicated. Sometimes you can like someone..."

"Love someone," Becky corrected.

"Sometimes you can love someone," I amended, "but it's just not the right time to be together."

"When is the right time?" Becky asked. "The boys here are mostly grown up. They don't need you to be home with them all the time or show up at every single sporting event, especially now that Luke and Lincoln can drive."

I looked around at the assembled faces at the table. "I'm really fine," I reiterated. I didn't know what else to say to make them feel better.

Leo leaned forward and grabbed my hand across the table. "I know better'n anyone in this room what it's like to find true love and then lose it. The angels took my Anna from me, and I didn't have a choice but to say goodbye."

His voice cracked as he continued, "You have a choice. Don't throw away love with a good man just because it's complicated to be together."

I jumped as I felt my phone buzzing in my pocket.

"Who's texting me?" I mused. "Almost everyone I know is right here."

My heart started pounding when I saw Martin's name on the screen. I swiped the screen and pulled up his message:

Weird question, but by any chance are you currently having an intervention?

Martin

My boys were circled around me in the living room, my sister and her boyfriend flanking them on either side.

"What if we all moved in with Lillian?" Charlie asked. "She's really cool for a girl. I can share a room with Logan and be his best friend."

Ever since that first day we got the kids together at Dave and Buster's, Charlie had a serious case of hero worship going on with Lillian's youngest. I was pretty sure it had something to do with Logan showing him how to beat his older brothers in one of the fantasy video games they all played. Mark and Karl were still trying to figure out that trick.

"Lillian's house isn't big enough for all of us to move in there," I answered.

"Then we'll just buy a new house," Mark said, as if it was that easy.

"If we moved to Kenilworth with the Wainwrights, y'all wouldn't be able to go to school here, you know. You'd have to leave all your friends and start fresh there."

"Daaad," Mark drew the word out to convey what an idiot I was. "First of all, there's technology now, you know, like cell phones and Facetime. Also, a lot of my friends are goin' to the other school, so I'm gonna need to make some new friends anyway."

We'd recently discovered that we were right over the boundary line for the junior high district, leaving my son separated from a good chunk of his sixth grade class.

"I don't mind changing' schools if I get to hang out with Logan and Luke and Linc," Charlie added. Karl and Mark nodded in agreement.

"But what about Aunt Maria?" I asked.

My sister rolled her eyes. When the intervention started, I assumed that she was the culprit, but then the boys explained that this had been their brilliant idea.

"You know I've been planning to move in with John anyway, and it's not like I can't drive over to Kenilworth to see you there."

"And you only have to go into your office once a week," Mark reminded me. "The rest of the time you're in the field or working' from home, so it won't be no problem for you to move either, Dad."

"Well, it sounds like y'all have figured out my whole life for me," I said.

"I wonder how it's going at Lillian's intervention," my sister whispered.

"What?"

I pulled out my phone, somehow unsurprised when Lillian responded immediately.

"Yeah, it's my first."

A corner of my mouth quirked up. I'd missed her sassy humor.

"See!" Maria jumped up, pointing her finger so close to my face she almost stabbed me in the nose. "That's the first time I've seen you smile since you broke up. You need to go talk to her. Now."

"Yeah, Dad," Mark piped up. "Aunt Maria will stay with us tonight. We'll see you tomorrow."

"Well, that's presumptuous," I grumbled.

I opened my message string with Lillian.

Any chance you'd be up for meeting at our usual place? The brew pub, I mean, not the Hotel Six. The terrorists holding me here say we need to talk. If we don't do it now, I have a feeling that they'll just find a way to Parent Trap us later.

Her response was immediate.

I'll leave now. See you there in a bit.

Fifteen minutes later I was waiting in the lobby of the brewpub, pacing nervously. I wasn't totally sure what I was going to say, but if our families and friends had gone through all the trouble of planning simultaneous interventions, I felt like we owed it to them to at least talk. And maybe we owed it to ourselves as well.

Lillian strode into the restaurant, looking like a woman on a mission. I took about ten seconds to categorize the gauntness that told me she hadn't been eating, and the dark circles around her eyes hinting at sleeplessness. Then I stalked across the lobby, grabbed her face between my hands, and kissed her. Hard.

She melted into me, opening her mouth with a sigh, and suddenly everything was right in my world again. I kissed her until someone cleared their throat loudly and when I ignored them, they tapped on my shoulder.

"Sir! Ma'am! Did y'all want to get a table? Or were you thinkin' you were at the Hotel Six up the street?"

Lillian grabbed my hand. "Let's get a table. We have a lot to talk about, and I'm suddenly starving. They didn't serve any food at my intervention."

"One star," I joked. "Don't recommend."

We were shown to a booth in the back and over double cheeseburgers, beer, and a huge basket of fries we shared our intervention stories.

"Lillian, I owe you an apology. I should have fought harder for us, not just gone along with breaking up."

She shook her head. "No, honestly I wasn't in a place to hear it then. My friend Becky thinks we gave up so easily because we'd both been abandoned by our partners in the past and, well, the truth is, despite what a pain in the ass it is with the distance and our schedules and everything, I feel like she might be right."

"What would you think about us moving to Kenilworth?"

"Us?"

"Me and the boys."

"You can't do that, Martin. They have school...and what about Maria? She's like a mother to them."

"I've been informed that they don't mind changing schools, and John's been pushing Maria to move in with him, so she's fine with it too."

Lillian stared at me for a long moment. "I don't feel right about asking you and your boys to give up your whole lives for us."

"We'd be doing it for 'us', all of us, not just your 'us'," I said.

She laughed. "That almost made sense. Are you sayin' that your boys *want* to change schools and move away Houston?"

I nodded. "They are surprisingly insistent about it, especially if it means they get to hang out with your boys more often. Charlie's got a plan to make Logan his best friend."

"Where would we live?" she asked, worrying her bottom lip. "I can't see us squeezing three more boys in my house."

"After we get married, we can sell our houses and buy something bigger. Or we can add an addition to your place or even build a bunk house in the back yard. Your yard is big enough to accommodate either option. I don't care where we live as long as we're together."

"After we get married?" I asked, latching onto the first part of that explanation.

"Why do you look so surprised? We talked about this at Dave and Buster's."

She rolled her eyes. "No, you and the boys talked about it. I don't recall you ever actually askin' me to get married."

"Do you want to get married?" I asked quickly, wanting to strike when the iron was hot.

"Well now, I don't know."

I could tell by the smirk on her face she was teasing me.

"Will it help if I get down on one knee?"

"Please don't," she laughed. "This is a big decision, you know. I mean, you're getting' quite a prize with me. It so happens I'm an incredible woman."

"That you are, my love."

"If we're gonna do this, I've got some conditions," she drawled.

"Such as?"

"I'm going to expect you to bring me coffee in the morning."

"Every day," I promised.

"And I enjoy having my own bathroom without hair in the sink and gross boy stuff everywhere."

"I promise to keep the gross boy stuff to a minimum, and I'll even promise to put the seat down every single time I pee."

"And I'm not running' a maid service. You and your kids are gonna be expected to do your share of the cooking' and cleaning', just like the rest of us."

"We do that now, so it's no problem," I assured her.

She raised her eyebrows. "You offer an attractive package of benefits, I'll give you that. It's very tempting."

"How about you accept my marriage proposal and then we'll go over to the Hotel Six and I'll offer you another attractive package."

I looked meaningfully down towards my lap, and she laughed.

"Miss!" she called. "Can we get the check please?"

Epilogue – Lillian

New Year's Eve...

"I don't know, should I have bought a new dress or something? Is it bad luck to get married in a dress you already had in your closet?"

I tugged at the skirt of the sparkly silver dress I'd worn last year on New Year's Eve. It was shocking how much had changed in one year. When Becky dragged me to that party last year, I never in a million years would have imagined falling in love with a guy and getting married.

Knowing that I was going to be a mom to six boys instead of three would have sent me away screaming. Even though the merging of our families had gone relatively smoothly, it wasn't without conflict.

And noise. Sweet baby Jesus, there was so much noise.

Martin sold his house in Houston surprisingly fast, and we'd use the proceeds to build an addition onto my house, adding two more bedrooms, another bathroom, and expanding both the kitchen and the family room. We'd all breathed a sigh of relief when it was finished and we could spread out a little.

I'd thought being the only female in a house with three males was bad but being in a house with seven? Let's just say we were ordering Febreze by the gallon and we now had two separate refrigerators to hold all the food these boys ate. Suffice it to say our grocery bill was astronomical. So was our water bill. And the electricity.

Even with Luke gone away to college last August, there were still a lot of expenses. Of course, he came home at least a couple of times a month anyway to do laundry and eat free food. Not that I minded.

"First of all, just like I told you last year, you look freakin' sexy as hell in that dress," Becky said as she curled my hair into some elaborate style. "Second, it's gonna be meaningful that you chose it to commemorate the night you fell in love."

Her voice got kind of dreamy when she said that, and I sent up a wish to the gods of relationships that my best friend would find something as good as what I found with Martin.

We were getting married in the same hotel we first met, the Ambassador Hotel in Houston. We'd reserved a small party room for the event and had only invited our closest friends and family.

Needless to say, my parents didn't make the cut. Two of my brothers had refused to attend to avoid any drama from my parents, but my brother Lewis and sister-in-law Sue were one of the first two people to accept the invitation. I appreciated their support.

Of course my found family was there too. Besides Becky I'd invited George and Cassie, Leo, Jimmy, Josie and David, and a few other friends and neighbors I'd been close to over the years.

Martin's parents were in attendance today. They were nice enough, but they were retired and traveled around a lot in their RV, so we didn't see them very often. Maria and John came, as well as a few of Martin's closer friends.

Becky had been tapped to be my maid-of-honor and Martin had asked his sister to be his 'best woman'. Both Becky and Maria were thrilled at the honor.

The hotel event planner popped in to tell us it was time to get started. I waited in the hallway, surprisingly calm, while Becky made her way up to the front of the room where the officiant and the rest of the wedding party waited.

I'd made Leo cry when I asked him to be our officiant. He'd taken one of those internet classes to get licensed to perform weddings, and he'd embraced his role with more excitement than I'd ever seen him display about anything other than football.

The wedding march started, and I entered the room. I could feel all eyes on me as I slowly walked up to Martin, but I didn't see anyone but him. When I reached the front, he pulled me into his arms.

"You wore my favorite dress!"

He sounded delighted.

"And you wore the same suit and tie you wore the night I met you," I said in amazement. "Great minds think alike."

"I guess it's true that we were meant to be, my love."

I blinked rapidly, trying hard not to cry. After all, I had a reputation as a badass to uphold. Plus, Becky had done my makeup and given me smoky eyes, and there was no way I wanted to look like a raccoon in our wedding pictures.

"Let's get married," I said softly. "Before one of our boys starts a belching contest or throws some food."

We both laughed as we turned to face Leo.

"You kids ready to get hitched?" he asked with a big smile on his face.

"We sure are."

***

Read all about how strong, silent George fell in love with efficiency expert Cassandra in "Factory Reset", available now at books2read.com/FactoryReset[1]

Want more midlife romance? You can get a free book when you join my newsletter. For more information, visit bit.ly/RoseBakNewsletter[2]

Hey there! If you liked this book, please show me some love, and leave a review. Good reviews are like puppies, they make everyone feel happy.

Keep reading for a special excerpt from "Summer Wedding[3]," available now.

---

1. https://books2read.com/FactoryReset

2. https://d.docs.live.net/ae511949052ccd53/Documents/bit.ly/RoseBakNewsletter

3.   https://books2read.com/u/bOzQ5g

Special Preview

Summer Wedding by Rose Bak

"Uncle Reed, when will you get here?"

I smiled at Jonathon's eager tone, even though he couldn't exactly see me through the car dashboard.

"I'm pulling into the parking lot now," I told him as I swung into an open parking spot that came up unexpectedly. "I'll…oh shit!"

"What's the matter?"

"I need to go, I'll call you when I'm checked in."

I clenched the steering wheel and took a deep breath, raising my head to look at the woman who was now on the hood of my car. The very angry woman. Our eyes met through the windshield and for a moment I lost my breath. She was beautiful.

Mentally shaking myself, I turned off the car and got out. My heart was racing. I couldn't believe I'd almost hit someone. I hadn't even seen her.

"I am so sorry. Are you okay? Do you need medical attention?"

The woman made to roll off the hood of the car and I rushed over to help her. I took her hand and everything inside me stilled. *Mine.* The word reverberated through my skull as what felt like an electrical current traveled between our palms.

"Careful," I said softly, my voice rough.

The woman stood up, brushing off her clothing. She was about my age, late forties or early fifties, with a trim, athletic figure. Faded jeans lovingly hugged her slim legs and narrow waist, and her tank top showed toned arms and generous breasts that I was itching to get my hands on. She had thick brown hair that fell past her shoulders in a cascade. Her eyes were chestnut brown, huge in her pale white face, and she had the cutest little button nose. And then there was her mouth...pouty thick lips, slick with some kind of gloss, and pressed together in a frown that told me she wasn't happy.

Oh yeah, probably because I'd hit her with my car.

"Are you okay?" I asked again. "I'm not sure what happened."

Her eyes narrowed in a glare.

"You were driving too fast and too busy talking on your phone to notice I was crossing through this parking space," she told me. "I jumped up on the hood to avoid being crushed."

She pointed at the car in the spot in front of me. There was maybe six inches between the bumper of that car and mine. Jesus. If she hadn't jumped up I might have crushed her. Whoever this woman was, she had good reflexes. I felt sick to my stomach at the idea that I could have seriously hurt her by not paying attention.

"Are you injured?" I asked.

She looked thoughtful and I had the sense she was doing a scan of her body for injuries.

"Probably bruised but nothing's broken, thank God."

"Let me make this right," I said, giving her a smile that had melted a lot of panties in my forty-nine years on this Earth. "Can I buy you dinner later? Or maybe a drink after you check in?"

Her spine snapped straighter, and she gave me a glare that could melt steel.

"Are you seriously hitting on me after you damn near ran me over?"

"Oh. Ah. No," I lied. "I just...what can I do to make it up to you?"

"Watch where you're going next time," she growled. "The next person you try to run over might not be as lucky."

She bent over to pick up the suitcase that she must've dropped when she was evading my car, and I absolutely did not check out her heart-shaped ass. Without another word, she started to walk away at a fast clip.

"At least let me give you my phone number," I said, jogging to catch up with her. "You can call me if you need anything."

She picked up her pace. "Leave me alone, asshole!"

Raising the middle finger of one hand over her shoulder to let me know what she thought of me, she stormed off towards the Main Lodge.

I sat back down in my car, feeling shaken. I couldn't decide if it was because of the near-miss of hitting the woman, or if it was my response to the woman herself. Even angry and flipping me off, there was something about her that called to me. I'd never felt this way about anyone before.

And you let her get away, dumbass, I told myself.

I gathered up my suitcase and headed into the lodge to check in, my pulse still racing. The woman was clearly staying here, so I'd just have to keep a look out for her. If we were meant to be – and I had no doubt that we were – fate would bring her to me again sooner or later.

***

For more of Reed and Erika's story check out Summer Wedding, available at select online retailers. For more information visit my website at bit.ly/AuthorRoseBak[1].

---

1. *https://books2read.com/ap/RDOk1w/Rose-Bak*

Other Books by Rose Bak

Boozy Book Club Series
Beach Reads
Bubbly & Billionaires
Martinis & Mysteries
Bourbon & Bikers
Midlife Madness
Extra Innings
The Marriage Solution
Midlife Crisis Contemporary Romance Series
Summer Wedding
Roasting with Rob
Christmas Punch
Disaster Planning
Factory Reset
Saving Texas
Texas Christmas
Second Chance to Score
Tempted at Midnight
The Good with Numbers Holiday Romance Series
Love Unmasked
The Thanksgiving Scrooge
Maid for Christmas
Countdown to Love
Valentine's Lottery
Christmas Angel
Loving the Holidays Contemporary Romance Series
Dating Santa
New Year's Steve
Independence Dave
Comfort & Joy

Faking It with the Detective
Dropping the Ball
Island Getaway
The Oliver Boys Band Contemporary Romance Series
Until You Came Along
Rock Star Teacher
Rock Star Writer
Rock Star Neighbor
Rock Star Lawyer
Magical Midlife Series
Beltane Magic (prequel)
Love Potion
Psychic Flashes
Halloween Surprise
Giant Love
Kitchen Magic
Alien Feeling
Bite-Sized Shifters Paranormal Romance Series
Long Distance Wolf
Wolf Doctor
Kat's Dog
Designer Wolf
Wolf Sheriff
Cocktail Wolf
Second Chance Wolf
Runaway Wolf
Holidays with the Shifters Series
Santa's Claws
Bear Humbug
Jingle Bear
Silver Paws
Joy to the Wolf

Lion's Heart
The Diamond Bay Contemporary Romance Series
Brand New Penny
Fresh as a Daisy
Right as Rain
Reunited Series
Together Again
Finding My Baby
King of the Reunion
Caught by My Best Friend
Standalones
Canadian Doctor
Beach Wedding
Jessie's Girl
Non-fiction
What to Do If You Find a Cougar in Your Living Room: Self-Care in an Uncaring World

It's All About Relationships: Reflections on Love, Friendship, and Connection

Catch up with these and other stories coming soon. Join my newsletter for more information[1] or follow my author page on your favorite retailer.

---

1.   *https://storyoriginapp.com/giveaways/62ee758e-068f-11eb-904e-c373f6014fe1*

About the Author

Rose Bak has been obsessed with books since she got her first library card at age five. She is a passionate reader with an e-reader bursting with thousands of beloved books.

Although Rose enjoys writing both fiction and nonfiction, romance novels have always been her favorite guilty pleasure, both as a reader and an author. Rose's contemporary romance books focus on strong female characters over thirty-five and the alpha males who love them. Expect a lot of steam, a little bit of snark, and a guaranteed happily ever after.

Rose lives in the Pacific Northwest with her family, and special needs dogs. In addition to writing, she also teaches accessible yoga and loves music. Sadly, she has absolutely no musical talent, so she mostly sings in the shower.

Please sign up for the Rose Bak Romance newsletter[1] to get a free book and keep up to date on all the latest news. You can also follow Rose on Facebook[2], Instagram[3], Twitter[4], Goodreads[5], or Bookbub[6].

---

1. https://storyoriginapp.com/giveaways/62ee758e-068f-11eb-904e-c373f6014fe1

2. https://www.facebook.com/AuthorRoseBak

3. https://www.instagram.com/authorrosebak/

4. https://twitter.com/AuthorRoseBak

5. https://www.goodreads.com/authorrosebak

6. https://www.bookbub.com/authors/rose-bak

Don't miss out!

Visit the website below and you can sign up to receive emails whenever Rose Bak publishes a new book. There's no charge and no obligation.

https://books2read.com/r/B-A-VATM-WBTSC

BOOKS 2 READ

Connecting independent readers to independent writers.

www.ingramcontent.com/pod-product-compliance
Lightning Source LLC
Chambersburg PA
CBHW051242160726
47994CB00002B/985